The Book Boat's In

by Cynthia Cotten

illustrated by Frané Lessac

Holiday House / New York

One sunny day, Jesse King and his pa drove into town.

As the wagon bumped along the main street, Jesse looked at all the boats tied up along the canal wharf.

All of a sudden, he grabbed Pa's sleeve. "Pa—stop!"

Pa reined in Jack, hard. "Good gravy, son," he said, "whatever is the matter?"

Jesse pointed at a long boat. On the side of the cabin was painted R. EDWARDS: LIBRARY AND BOOKSTORE. "The book boat's in," he said. "Can I go?"

Pa nodded. "Go on," he said. "I'll come get you soon's I get that new ax handle."

Jesse jumped down and took off running to the wharf.

Mr. Edwards was just hanging up a sign that said OPEN. "Whoa there," he said as Jesse bounded over the gangplank and onto the deck. "You know the rule."

LIBRARY AND BOOKSTORE

Jesse rubbed his hands hard
on his pants, then held them out.
    "Hmm." Mr. Edwards inspected
them, palms and backs.
    Jesse held his breath.
    Mr. Edwards grinned.
"You'll do. Go on in."

Inside, the walls of the cabin were lined with shelves full of books. Chairs were placed near the windows so folks could sit and read. A table held more books.

Jesse loved books. He'd read every single one on the shelf behind Miss Howard's desk at school, some of them twice. As he browsed, a red cover on the table caught his eye. He picked up the book. *The Swiss Family Robinson*. Of all Miss Howard's books, this was his favorite, a story of shipwreck and adventure.

"How much for this?" he asked.

"Twenty cents," Mr. Edwards said. "And worth every penny. It's been read some, but it's in real good condition."

"Jesse?" Pa poked his head into the cabin. "Time to go."
Jesse showed him the book. "Look, Pa. It's a real good one."
Pa shook his head. "Not today. That ax handle cost more
than I thought it would."

Jesse ran his fingers over the red cover, then put the book
on the table. "When will you be back?" he asked Mr. Edwards.

"A week from today," Mr. Edwards said. "And that'll be it for a good while."

"I'd sure like to have that book for my own," Jesse said as the wagon jounced toward home.

"Maybe you could earn some money before the boat comes back," Pa said. "Ask around."

Back home, Jesse climbed up to his sleeping loft and took his treasure box from a little shelf nailed to the wall. In the box was a sparkly stone, a brass button with an eagle on it, and a little leather pouch that held three copper pennies—two he'd earned picking apples and one he'd found on the street—and a silver dime given to him on his tenth birthday by Grandfather King. Thirteen cents. He needed seven more.

On Monday, after school, Jesse went to the general
store. "Do you have any work I could do?" he asked the
owner, Mrs. Blake.

She thought for a moment. "I haven't had time
to sweep the floor today," she said.

"I can do that," Jesse said. Jesse swept every inch of the store's floor. He even swept the porch and wiped the front windows with a rag he found behind the counter. When he was finished, Mrs. Blake paid him a penny for the sweeping and an extra halfpenny for the windows.

Jesse worked every day after school. He cleaned harnesses
at the livery stable, chopped wood for the tavern, and ran two
errands for Dr. Porter.

When he went home, he had chores and studying to do. There was no time to play. But Jesse didn't mind. By the end of the week, he had seventeen and a half cents.

"It's not near enough," he told Ma. "But maybe if I tell Mr. Edwards how hard I've worked, he'll sell me the book for that much."

Saturday morning, after breakfast, Jesse said, "Can we go into town?"

"Chores first," Pa said. "There are potatoes to be dug and stones to be cleared from that patch I want to plant next."

Jesse worked all morning and into the afternoon, stopping only for a short noon meal. At last Pa said, "That's enough for today. Let's wash, and I'll hitch up Jack."

Jesse scrubbed his hands and face. He stuffed the leather pouch into his pocket, then climbed up on the wagon seat beside Pa.

All the way to town, Jesse felt fidgety, inside and out. What if the boat didn't come today? What if it had already come and gone? "Can't Jack go any faster?" he asked.

"Don't worry," Pa said, patting Jesse's knee. "We'll get there."

OPEN R. EDWARDS

When they got to town, Jesse raced down to the wharf. There was the book boat, and Mr. Edwards talking to one of the dockhands.

"Catch your breath, son," Mr. Edwards said. "I'm here until tomorrow. Let's see your hands."

Jesse held out his hands.

"All right," Mr. Edwards said. "Go on in. I'll be right there."

Jesse went straight to the table. But the red-covered book wasn't there. Not on the table, not on the shelves.

"Mr. Edwards," he said, "the book I wanted—where is it?"

"Gone," Mr. Edwards said. "I sold it yesterday."

Jesse turned his head, squeezing back tears. After all his hard work?

"How about this instead?" Mr. Edwards pulled a brown-covered book from beneath the counter.

Jesse shook his head. "No, thanks."

"Just take a look."

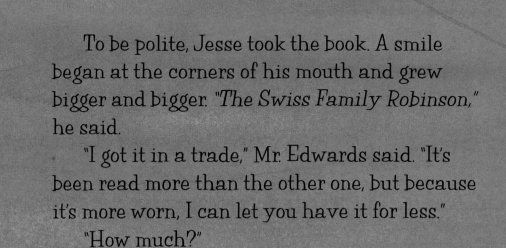

To be polite, Jesse took the book. A smile began at the corners of his mouth and grew bigger and bigger. *The Swiss Family Robinson,*" he said.

"I got it in a trade," Mr. Edwards said. "It's been read more than the other one, but because it's more worn, I can let you have it for less."

"How much?"

Mr. Edwards rubbed his chin. "How does fourteen cents sound?"

"Done!" Jesse counted fourteen cents into Mr. Edwards's hand. "Thank you," he added.

Mr. Edwards put the money in a little box. Then he pushed a quill pen and a little bottle of ink across the counter. "Better put your name in it," he said.

Jesse dipped the quill into the ink. Opening the book, he wrote inside the cover, *Jesse King. His book, 1835.*

AUTHOR'S NOTE

I first learned about floating libraries when I read a newspaper article written by Doug Farley, director of the Erie Canal Discovery Center in my hometown of Lockport, New York.

As I read it, I thought back to my younger days and remembered the first time I saved my money and bought a book of my own. It was a novel titled *The Travels of Jaimie McPheeters*, by Robert Lewis Taylor. I still have it.

When the Erie Canal was finished in 1825, it opened the door to westward expansion. Boats of all kinds traveled up the Hudson River from New York City to Albany, then west to Lake Erie and beyond. Cities such as Buffalo, Cleveland, Chicago, and Detroit grew rapidly. Many people continued even farther west by land.

There were packet boats and line boats that carried people, and freighters that delivered grain, lumber, and other cargo. And for a number of years, floating libraries brought learning and culture to people who would otherwise have had little access to books. Back and forth across the state they went—spring, summer, and fall—stopping only during the winter months, when the canal was closed to traffic. These boats carried all kinds of books between Albany and Buffalo, stopping at towns along the way, sometimes for just a few hours, sometimes for a few days. A person could either rent a book for a small fee, keeping it until the boat came back, or buy a book outright.

As many towns along the canal grew, they built their own free libraries. Eventually, the book boats vanished. But for a time they provided an invaluable service to many people—including young ones like Jesse.

For every librarian we have ever known—
and those we have yet to meet
—C. C. & F. L.

The illustrator would like to give special thanks
to Matthew Reeves, aka Jesse,
and Dan Ward, Curator of the Erie Canal Museum.

Text copyright © 2013 by Cynthia Cotten
Illustrations copyright © 2013 by Frané Lessac
All Rights Reserved
HOLIDAY HOUSE is registered in the U.S. Patent and Trademark Office.
Printed and Bound in October 2012 at Tien Wah Press, Johor Bahru, Johor, Malaysia.
The text typeface is Happy.
The artwork was created with gouache on Arches paper.
www.holidayhouse.com
First Edition
1 3 5 7 9 10 8 6 4 2

Library of Congress Cataloging-in-Publication Data
Cotten, Cynthia.
The book boat's in / by Cynthia Cotten ; illustrated by Frané Lessac. — 1st ed.
p. cm.
Summary: On a book boat on the Erie Canal in the 1800s, Jessie spots a used copy of
The Swiss Family Robinson, then works very hard all week to earn the money he needs to buy it.
Includes historical note.
ISBN 978-0-8234-2521-1 (hardcover)
[1. Books and reading—Fiction. 2. Libraries—Fiction.
3. Erie Canal (N.Y.)—History—19th century—Fiction.]
I. Lessac, Frané, ill. II. Title. III. Title: Book boat is in.
PZ7.C82865Boo 2013
[E]—dc23 `
2012016548